∞

The Magical Day

by Sandra Elaine Scott

THE MAGICAL DAY

PUBLISHED BY VISION YOUR DREAMS

PRINTED IN THE UNITED STATES OF AMERICA
This book is a work of fiction. Names, characters, places, and incidents either are products of the author's imagination or are used fictitiously. Any resemblance to actual persons, living or dead, events, or locales is entirely coincidental.

Library of Congress Control Number: 2015918248
ISBN-10:0996904905
ISBN-13:978-0-9969049-0-2

Author's Photographs ~ Arlene Lagos
Book Design ~ Karen White
Illustrations ~ Jasmine Mills

Visit website at: www.visionyourdreams.com

This book is dedicated to
Damiela y Damael

Thanks for a Magical Summer

Table of Contents

Chapter One
The Plane Ride

Donovan was excited and scared all at the same time. He was on his way to the States to visit with his aunt and cousin for summer vacation.

"Don't worry," Donovan's father said. "Mama and your new little sister will be just fine. She just needs to rest and wants you to have fun this summer."

Donovan hugged his dad. He boarded the plane with the friendly flight attendant who asked him if this was his first plane ride.

"This is my first plane ride without my parents," he responded. "I am going to stay with my aunt and cousin for the summer." After the plane took off, they continued to chat. Time flew by, and the next thing Donovan knew she was telling him to prepare for the landing.

When Donovan got off the plane, he spotted his aunt and pointed to her excitedly.

"There she is! That's my Tía Vivia and my cousin, Maria Luisa!"

"Your aunt is just like you described her," said the flight attendant.

Donovan's aunt had freckles and her springy red hair had curls that went every which way. Donovan stared at Tía. He was overjoyed to see her.

"I am so glad you are here," she smiled. "Are you ready to have a magical summer?"

"Mama said you are weird," Donovan said innocently. Tía Vivia let out a belly laugh and wiped tears of laughter from her eyes. "My sister always said that I was the weird one. Come, let's get you home and settled in."

Chapter Two
Settling In

Donovan's cousin, Maria Luisa, chatted the whole ride. "Donovan, when we visited you in Jamaica you showed me around. Now it's my turn and I can't wait. I told everybody in the neighborhood that you were coming and tomorrow we are going to…"

"Shush! Maria Luisa, remember it's a surprise," her mother cut in.

"Surprise?" said Donovan. "What kind of surprise?"

"Never you mind, nosey one. Let's get you home, and then maybe I'll let Maria Luisa tell you," chuckled Tía Vivia.

Later that evening after dinner, Tía Vivia turned to her daughter and said, "Now you can tell the big secret."

"Well Donovan, tomorrow we are going on an adventure! Just you and me! We are going to spend time with my favorite people. Mama will not even tell me how we are going to do it, but she promises that tomorrow morning,

we will learn about it together," Maria Luisa announced dramatically.

"Yes, Maria Luisa, if I had told you, you wouldn't have been able to keep it a secret. Now it's time for both of you to get ready for bed. You have a big day tomorrow," laughed Tía Vivia.

8

Chapter Three
The Big Day

The next morning, Donovan looked into his cousin's room and saw his aunt taking her temperature.

"Oh Donovan!" Maria Luisa wailed. "Mama says I can't get out of bed. I have a fever and the sniffles, so she won't let me go."

Maria Luisa continued to whine. "But Mama, I feel fine."

Donovan's Tía firmly shook her head, "No, absolutely not. You will stay in bed until you feel better. I will be back to keep you company."

Tía Vivia gently steered Donovan into the kitchen. "Cheer up," she told him. "I promise you, you will still have a magical day."

After breakfast, Tía asked Donovan to get the Treasure Box from the living room. Tía encouraged Donovan to open it.

He peeked inside and his eyes got bigger and bigger. "What is this?" he asked, as he pulled

out a map that looked like a huge figure eight with names on it.

"Today, you will meet some of our special neighborhood friends. Everyone is excited to meet you."

Lips quivering, Donovan replied, "But I can't do this by myself, not without Maria Luisa showing me where to go."

"Of course you can. They are just down the street" answered Tía. "All you have to do is believe."

"Believe what?" Donovan asked.

Tía Vivia gently grabbed his hand and held it over his heart. "Believe here, inside of you, that there is all this magic, and you hold the key to do it."

As Donovan's Tía prepared him for his journey, she silently said a prayer to bless his day. She gave him a big hug and watched him walk towards the fire station.

Chapter Four
The Firefighter

Donovan started his adventure. He looked at his map and slowed his steps as he neared the firehouse. There were a lot of firefighters standing outside and he was nervous.

"Hey, are you our new fire recruit?" shouted the biggest man he had ever seen. With a big gulp, Donovan shook his head, "No, I am looking for Firefighter Joey."

The firefighter let out a huge laugh. "Well you found him. Come on in! You are my new recruit, and I am making you an honorary firefighter."

"I can't be a firefighter," Donovan said in a small voice. "I'd be too scared to do anything like that."

Firefighter Joey leaned closer to him and whispered, "You know what? Me too!"

Donovan's eyes widened as big as saucers. "You get scared? I don't believe it," he said.

"I sure do get scared! But I also know that people are counting on me. When I am really

scared, I think about lions and how they protect their pride and how brave they are. So in the moment, I am no longer scared. I am brave like a lion."

"Have you ever visited a fire station before?" asked the firefighter. Donovan shook his head. The firefighter introduced him to the other firefighters and gave him a tour of the station.

Pointing toward the nearby community garden, Firefighter Joey said, "I know you are meeting Mr. Johnson next. Now, you know that you can go out there and be a little scared because that is what makes you very brave." With that, Firefighter Joey sent Donovan on his way.

As Donovan continued down the road, he knew that he was going to be just like Firefighter Joey, a little scared and very brave.

Chapter Five
The Gardener

Donovan arrived at the community garden minutes later and looked at the growing vegetables. He spotted Mr. Johnson kneeling over a plant.

Mr. Johnson invited him to get down with him in the dirt and help him plant.

"Mr. Johnson, why do you do this?" Donovan asked. Mr. Johnson smiled and snapped off a sugar pea pod. He encouraged Donovan to taste it.

Donovan looked skeptical, scrunched his face, shrugged his shoulders, but ate it.

"How does that taste?" Mr. Johnson asked.

"It's sweet!" Donovan said, surprised.

Mr. Johnson laughed. "My boy, that's why I love to garden. There is no greater joy than to plant something, take care of it every day, and watch it grow. It makes me happy that I can share it with my friends. Planting in the community garden is something that I can do for the entire neighborhood. I am doing something

useful and with a little time and effort, and a little love, I get to share this gift and that makes it worth it!"

Mr. Johnson gave Donovan a seedling and helped him plant it. "See, Donovan," he said, "now you have a memory of this day, and with a little luck, it will be a joy worth sharing." Mr. Johnson gave him a small bag filled with vegetables to take home.

"Thank you, Mr. Johnson," said Donovan. He loaded his backpack and headed to his next stop.

Chapter Six
The Soldier

Donovan looked at his map and saw a flag. As he neared the building, he saw about a dozen service men and women loading crates into trucks.

Bravely, he asked for the Commander. One person pointed to a very tall man who seemed to be yelling at people to move boxes and to hurry up. He started to feel a little scared once again.

The Commander looked over and in midsentence broke into a huge smile. "Why, you must be Donovan," he said.

Donovan stared but nothing came out of his mouth.

"The cat got your tongue, son?" barked the Commander.

"No, I mean, uh yes," stammered Donovan.

"Which is it?" the Commander laughed. "Are you or are you not Donovan?"

The other service members reassured Donovan. "He's just teasing you," one said.

"Come on over and tell me about yourself," said Commander Mitchell, patting the seat next to one he had taken.

Donovan sat down. The Commander told him that he was glad that he and Maria Luisa were helping out.

"Thank you so much for agreeing to write to our service men and women overseas. They will really appreciate receiving a letter. It means so much to them."

"Really?" said Donovan, sounding surprised. "They want letters and cards from kids? I would think they would want something else."

The Commander looked him in the eye. "They are proud to serve their country. Every day they do an important job that helps keep us safe. They are grateful to all the kids who take the time to write to them, because it shows that they care. So you, Mr. Donovan, stand tall and proud. You are a fine young man, and on behalf of all those who serve, I thank you."

The Commander let him know that there would be almost 70 service members who would receive their letters. The busy service members called out to thank Donovan as he left the post with his head a little higher. He walked on to his next stop tall and proud.

Church

24

Chapter Seven
The Nun

Donovan's map pointed him towards the church. His steps slowed as he neared the doors. He was thinking that he wasn't dressed for church, and wasn't sure that his Tía meant to include this on his trip. Just as he reached the door, he bumped into a nun coming out.

"Oh, my goodness, you must be Donovan," she said.

Donovan nodded. "Speak up! I am getting too old to interpret head nods," she said with a huge smile.

This immediately put Donovan at ease. "You must be Sister Mary Magdalene," said Donovan.

"Yes, but your cousin calls me Sister M&M." She invited Donovan to take a seat on the bench beside her. She sensed Donovan was a little worried about something. Sister Mary Magdalene peered at Donovan. "You look like you want to ask me something."

"Do you think my mom and my sister are okay?" Donovan asked.

Sister Mary Magdalene said thoughtfully, "Some nights you do not see the moon and you know it's up there. And on cloudy days, you don't see the sun, but you know that it rises every single day. Faith is like that. Faith is believing in what we cannot see. Just because we don't see something, or can't touch it, doesn't mean that it's not true."

Sister Mary Magdalene took his hand, placed it over his heart. "Let's pray," she said. "Today we are grateful that you are visiting with us for the summer. We have faith that your family at home is well and waiting joyously for you to come home."

Donovan's face split into a huge smile as he thanked her. She blessed him and sent him off to see her friend around the building.

Chapter Eight
The Graffiti Artist

"Hey, little man! You must be the helper Sister told me I was going to have for the afternoon." Giving Donovan a high five, he said, "I'm Enrique. Good to meet you."

"What are you doing?" asked Donovan.

"Well right now, I am using my creative talents for good, or so says Sister Mary Magdalene," Enrique laughed. "Do you like to paint?"

"Well, I do it at school," said Donovan. "But I am not very good."

"I bet you are really good at it, but you just don't know it. Come on, you are going to help me. I want you to put your hands in the paint. I'm going to turn up the music, and I want you to dance on the wall with your fingers and see what you come up with."

Donovan looked a little doubtful. "That's crazy, but it sounds fun," he said.

With the music pumping, they both started to dance with their fingers dripping in paint, and the more they moved, the more they laughed.

Finally, out of breath, Donovan looked at the wall and loved the huge splash of color that went in every direction.

As they cleaned up, Enrique admired Donovan's work.

"Donovan, you are an artist. Look at the wonderful piece of art you created!"

Donovan waved goodbye to Enrique. He had so much fun being creative that he went bopping down the street to the rhythm of the music.

Chapter Nine
The Athlete

Donovan turned the corner onto a basketball court and came upon a girl his age in a wheelchair. "Are you Sally Anne?" he asked, "I'm Donovan."

"Uh huh," she said without taking her eyes off the ball she was shooting into the hoop. He watched her for a while and asked. "Don't you ever get tired?"

"Nope," she replied. "I'm trying out for the Olympics."

"The Olympics?" he asked in amazement.

Donovan looked at her sideways. He did not want to make her mad, but couldn't stop from asking "But how? You're in a wheelchair," he sputtered.

"Yeah, I know that. Actually the Paralympics are for kids who are differently abled like me! Don't you know that you can do anything that you want to do?" she sighed.

"I am a good basketball player and I am going to be great," she said as she shot the ball.

"You can?" as he stared at her in disbelief.

"Yeees. ...All you have to do is try and never give up. That's what my parents tell me every day and so does my basketball coach. I'm going to be in the Olympics. So every day, I try as hard as I can, and work as hard as I can."

Donovan looked at her wide-eyed. He had never heard a kid speak that way. All he could say was, "Really?"

"Sure," said Sally Anne as she passed him the ball, "Come on! Let's play! Just do your best, keep trying, and don't quit!"

When they finished playing, Donovan left smiling, thinking that if she never gives up, then he shouldn't either.

Chapter Ten
The Librarian

Donovan got to the last destination on his map. It was also his favorite, the library. He loved story time and couldn't wait to go in. As he walked through the doors, he smiled and headed to the children's section.

"Excuse me, are you Miss Lily?"

"You must be Donovan," said Miss Lily. "Where is Maria Luisa?" she asked.

"She is sick so I came by myself."

"You did? Wow! Such a brave young man you are to come by yourself! Well, let's get some books for you and your cousin."

Donovan chatted with Miss Lily, telling her about all the things he loved to read. He loved spooky adventure stories and wanted a book that he and Maria Luisa could read together.

He asked Miss Lily if the library had books in Spanish.

"Wow! You speak Spanish, too?" she asked surprised.

"Yes," he said, "but I don't read it well. Mama makes me get books in both languages."

"You are a bright little boy, Donovan. I can only speak one language and you speak two. That's cool!" said Miss Lily.

After Donovan chose some books, Miss. Lily said to him again. "Donovan, you are smart. You and your cousin can teach me a few words in Spanish."

He laughed. "Soon, you will be like my dad and speak a little Spanglish." He waved goodbye to Miss Lily, saying "Adios!" as he left.

Chapter Eleven
Happy Day!

Walking back to his aunt's house, Donovan noticed people waving and smiling at him. He didn't remember seeing any other people when he started out that morning, but his parents always told him to be polite. So he waved and smiled back at everyone.

When he reached the house, the door flew open. His Tía greeted him saying, "Maria Luisa has been bursting at the seams waiting for you!"

"How is she feeling?"

"She is feeling much better and cannot wait to hear about your adventures."

Donovan ran down the hall. "I had so much fun, and I wish you had been with me," he yelled to Maria Luisa.

He spread out his map and excitedly recounted his day with Firefighter Joey, Mr. Johnson, Colonel Mitchell, Sister M&M, Enrique, Sally Anne, and Miss Lily. Donovan and Maria Luisa compared notes about the wonderful people he had met.

Tía Vivia stood in the doorway amazed at the change in Donovan. She smiled and was thankful to all who had helped make his day a great one.

Donovan glanced over and saw his Tía's smiling face. He ran over, grabbed her by the waist, and gave her a big hug.

"Tía, Tía," he exclaimed, "Yes, indeed it was a Magical Day!"

What Donovan Learned About His Friends on His Magical Day

To Find Joy

To Be Brave

To Be Proud

To Be Creative

To Be Smart

To Have Faith

To Never Give Up

Miss Lily's Spanish Words

Tía ~ Aunt

Adios ~ Goodbye

Spanglish ~ Mixing Spanish and English together that is not quite English, not quite Spanish.

Cool Sites to Help You Create Your Own Magical Days

NVFC National Junior Firefighter
http://juniors.nvfc.org

Kids Gardening
http://www.kidsgardening.org

NGA Kids—
National Gallery of Art
www.nga.gov/kids/kids.htm

Paralympics
http://www.paralympic.org

Children's Book Week
http://www.bookweekonline.com

Wicked Awesome!

Thanks so much to everyone who helped make this book a success. A high five to all my early readers with their valuable feedback. A great big hug to these amazing individuals for their insight: Bernadette, Darryl, Gladys, and Sheri. Special shout-out to my niece, Natalie Rowe, who reminded me "They're Kids." Thanks also to my amazing team of editors: Sandra James and Grammar Goddess Susan Rooks. And of course, this book would be incomplete without the fantastic artwork from Jasmine Mills and the book design of Karen White.

But you know what...I thank God most of all for the 4:00-in-the-morning dream and the nudge to wake up and write. I found joy with two amazing young friends, Damiela y Damael, who showed up at my door making me smile each day. I learned to be brave as I shared my idea for this story with all the amazing people I met. They walked the magical road with me. They held my hand when I was nervous and most of all encouraged me to keep going. I am proud that I got to share a little bit of my culture, and most of all I had so much fun creating my own magical day.

Muchísimas Gracias

Miss Sandra

About the Author

Sandra Elaine Scott is an award-winning author and a child at heart. Inspired by a dream, she shares the uplifting tale of Donovan in *The Magical Day* using her own bicultural heritage and her love for diversity as a backdrop. Sandra's wish is that all children learn to have faith in themselves and are empowered to create their own magical days. To contact Miss Sandra email her at **sandra@visionyourdreams.com**

CPSIA information can be obtained
at www.ICGtesting.com
Printed in the USA
BVOW05*2057281117

501379BV00014B/38/P

9 780996 904902